Fairy Tales
for Little Children

Fairy Tales
for Little Children
Illustrated by Lorena Alvarez
Retold by Susanna Davidson

Contents

Little Red Riding Hood

Once upon a time,
there was a little girl called
Little Red Riding Hood
who always wore a ruby-red cloak.

She lived near a **deep, dark** *forest*,

where her mother kept bees...

...and her *father* chopped down trees.

One day, Little Red Riding Hood's mother gave her a pot of honey. "Please will you take this to Grandma, on the other side of the forest."

Little Red Riding Hood skipped through the forest, singing a little song.

"I'm so happy with the birds and the bees,
Nothing's going to happen to me in these trees."

"Hello!" called her father, as she skipped along. "Hello!" sang Little Red Riding Hood, in reply.

But someone else was watching
Little Red Riding Hood.
Can you see who it is?

That's right. It's a WOLF!
A little girl! How delicious!
How I'd love to GOBBLE her up!

Nor was this just any old wolf. Oh no. This was a **crafty**, **clever**, **cunning** wolf... who loved to *set* **TRAPS**.

The wolf quickly hung a net beneath a tree and waited as Little Red Riding Hood came closer and **closer** and **closer**...

...until **skippety-skippety-SKIP...**

...*she sailed right over the net.*

"RATS!"

snarled the wolf.

The wolf raced ahead and dug a large hole in the ground, then covered it in leaves.

Skippety-skippety-*skip*...
Little Red Riding Hood came **closer** and **closer** and **closer**...

...until she skipped right over the hole.
The wolf pounced... and missed.

"RATS!" he hissed.

"Time for my last plan," said the wolf. And, grinning and giggling, he raced to Grandma's cottage and knocked on the door.

He waited *for* Grandma to come to the door...

...then he
gobbled her
up in one
hungry gulp.

"Now *for* dessert,"
chuckled the wol*f*.

He pulled on Grandma's clothes, leaped into bed, and waited some more...

At last, there came a **tap** at the door.

"Oh Grandma!" said Little Red Riding Hood, skipping into the room. "There's something different about you today."

"What big **EARS** you have!" said Little Red Riding Hood, coming closer.

"All the better to **HEAR** you with," said the wolf.

Little Red Riding Hood had come closer still.
"All the better to **SEE** you with," said the wolf.

"What big, hairy **HANDS** you have,"
said Little Red Riding Hood.

"All the better to **HUG** you with,"
replied the wolf. And he grinned.

"Oh! What big **TEETH** you have."

"All the better to **EAT YOU** with," cried the wolf.

In one bound, the wolf leaped out of bed and **GOBBLED** up Little Red Riding Hood.

Then he went to *sleep*
with a *full* tummy...

...and a VERY *satisfied* smile on his whiskery *face.*

But the wolf didn't realize that this time HE was being watched.

Little Red Riding Hood's *father* **smashed** his way into the cottage.

He took one look at the wolf's big belly, grabbed some scissors and snipped him open.

Out popped
Little Red Riding Hood
AND her Grandma.

Now it was Grandma who had a **crafty**, **clever**, **cunning** idea.

"Run outside," she said to Little Red Riding Hood.

"And *fetch* me some nice round pebbles."

Then she dropped the pebbles into the wolf's tummy... and stitched him up.

When the wolf woke up, he clutched his belly and howled and howled and **HOWLED** again.

He ran outside, the stones rattling
and clattering inside him.

"I'll never be able to gobble up a human ever again!" he moaned.

"Everyone will hear me coming."

As *for* Little Red Riding Hood... she went **skippety-skippety-skip** all the way home, her ruby-red cloak swishing and swaying behind her...

Goldilocks and the Three Bears

There was once a naughty little girl called

Goldilocks.

Was she naughty once a month?
Or once a week?

No! That wasn't enough *for* Goldilocks.

She liked to do something naughty EVERY DAY...

...and every night too.

She never, **ever** did as she was told!

One day, Goldilocks' mother asked her to go to the village to buy some bread.

"Go straight there and come straight back again," she said.

Did Goldilocks do as she
was told? Of course not!

Instead she wandered
this way and that...

...until she came to a little cottage.

Goldilocks crept up to the window and peered *inside*.

"No one home!" she giggled...

...and pushed open the *front* door. "Mmm," said Goldilocks.

Inside, was the most **delicious** smell.

"It's **PORRIDGE!**" cried Goldilocks, gazing greedily at the table.

First, she tried the
great big bowl.

Too hot!

Next, she tried the
middle-sized bowl.

Too cold!

Last of all,
she tried the
teeny tiny bowl.

"Yum," said Goldilocks.

"This porridge is JUST RIGHT."

And she ate it ALL UP.

Slurp! Burp!

"What next?" wondered Goldilocks.

"I think I'll *sit* by the *fire*."

And she climbed into a **great big** rocking chair.

"Oh it's
TOO HARD!"
said Goldilocks.

"I know! I'll try the
middle-sized chair."

But the middle-sized
chair was TOO SOFT.

"Oh look!" cried Goldilocks.

"A teeny
tiny
little
baby
chair."

"And it's
JUST RIGHT!"

But no sooner had Goldilocks sat down than there was a loud **SNAP** as the chair **CRACKED!**

"Oh dear," said Goldilocks.

"Never mind! I'll go upstairs and have a lovely little nap."

In the bedroom, there were three beds.

First, Goldilocks tried the

GREAT
BIG
BED.

"TOO HARD," she said.

Next, she tried the middle-sized bed.

"TOO SOFT," she said.

Last of all, she tried the teeny tiny bed.

"JUST RIGHT," said Goldilocks.
And she closed her eyes and fell fast asleep.

As Goldilocks slept,
three bears came
to the house.

There was a great big father bear,
a middle-sized mother bear
and a teeny, tiny baby bear.

They had been on a long walk and
they were all three VERY hungry.

"Who's been eating MY porridge?" growled Father Bear.

"Who's been eating MY porridge?" grumbled Mother Bear.

"Someone's been eating MY porridge too," squeaked Baby Bear.

"AND THEY'VE EATEN IT ALL UP."

Next, Father Bear went over to the *fire*.

"Who's been *sitting* in MY chair?" he *growled*.

Mother Bear was right behind him.

"Who's been *sitting* in MY chair?" *she said*.

"Someone's been *sitting* in MY chair," wailed Baby Bear,

"AND THEY'VE BROKEN IT!"

Then came the *sound* of loud *snores from* the bedroom. The three bears climbed the *stairs*.

"Who's been *sleeping* in MY bed?" grumbled Father Bear.

"Who's been *sleeping* in MY bed?"
growled Mother Bear.

"Someone's been *sleeping* in MY bed,"
cried Baby Bear. "And *she's* **STILL** there!"

Goldilocks woke up, took one look at the

great big father bear,

middle-sized mother bear

and *tiny*, little baby bear

and she **SCREAMED!**

She ran all the way home, *saying*...

"...I'll never,
EVER be
naughty
again."

And she
ALMOST
never was...

Jack and the Beanstalk

Once upon a time, there was a brave, bold, adventurous boy called **Jack**.

He and his mother were

VERY,

VERY

poor.

"We have no money left,"
said his mother, one day.

"All we have is our cow. You must take her to market and sell her. It's our last hope."

On the way to market,
Jack met a strange little man,
dancing by the side of the path.

Hello, Young Man!
Would you like to sell me your cow?

“In return
I can offer you
FIVE
MAGIC
BEANS.”

If you plant them, they'll grow into a beanstalk that can touch the sky!

So Jack gave the man his cow and ran home with the MAGIC beans.

"A beanstalk..." he whispered to himself. "That can touch the sky! Mother will be..."

"FURIOUS!" cried his mother.
"I'm FURIOUS!
We need MONEY, not BEANS!"

And she threw the beans
out of the window.

Jack went to bed full of gloom.
"I should have known there's
no such thing as magic."

But the next morning, when Jack looked out of his window, he was met with a sea of green.

There, like a ladder to the clouds, was the beanstalk, twisting and turning above him.

I wonder where it goes?

Unable to resist, Jack began to climb.

He climbed up
and up
and up,
past *flying* birds,
through misty clouds,
until he reached a castle
at the very top.

And there,
on the castle
doorstep, was a
GIANTESS!

"Excuse me," called Jack.

"Could I possibly have some breakfast?"

The giantess picked Jack up
and dangled him before her eyes.

"You're very brave and bold.
Don't *you* know my husband
would eat YOU *for* breakfast?"

"You can come *inside*,"
said the giantess...

"But you'd better be *gone* by
the time he *gets* home."

Jack munched his way
through MOUNTAINS
of bread and CHUNKS
of cheese.

But then there came a

STOMP!

STOMP!

STOMP!

"Quick!" said the giantess. "Hide in here." And she popped Jack into the sugar pot...

...just as a GIANT strode into the kitchen.

Fee! Fi! Fo! Fum! I smell the blood of an Englishman. Be he alive or be he dead, I'll grind his bones to make my bread!

"WHERE IS HE?" shouted the giant.
"There's no one here," said his wife.

"You must be imagining things."

"Then bring me my golden hen!"
demanded the giant.

The giant looked at the hen and roared,
"LAY, hen, LAY!"
To Jack's amazement, the hen
laid an egg of solid gold.

Soon after,
the giant fell
fast asleep.

"Run, Jack, run!"
whispered
the giantess.

But Jack
wasn't going
ANYWHERE
without the
golden hen.

He grabbed the hen and bolted for the door. "SQUAWK! SQUAWK!" went the golden hen.

The giant woke up and cried:

"AFTER HIM!"

Jack raced through the castle.
The giant raced after Jack.

STOMP! STOMP!
STOMP!

As the giant came down the beanstalk,
it began to bend and sway.

"I'm going to CRUNCH you and
MUNCH you," roared the giant.

Clutching the hen, Jack called
down to his mother,
"Fetch the axes!"

There's a GIANT after me!

As soon as Jack reached the bottom, he and his mother hacked away at the beanstalk...

...until it came **CRASHING** to the ground.

The giant was *flung* into the deep beyond, never to return.

As for Jack and his
mother, they lived
happily ever after.
Aren't we lucky to
have a golden hen.
Although, sometimes,
Jack would dream
of climbing a
beanstalk again...

Cinderella

Once upon a *fairy* tale, there was a girl called **Cinderella**.

Did *she* have a happy life? **NO!**

She had to cook and clean all day long.

Cinderella lived with her **horrid** stepmother and her two **grisly** stepsisters.

They *slept* in four poster beds on *silken* *sheets*.

Poor Cinders *slept* by the *fire*.

What's for supper?

Where's our lunch?

Cinderella was bossed about *from* dawn till dusk. But she never snapped or said an unkind word.

Then one day, an
invitation arrived.
It was *for* the
Royal Ball.

Of course you can't go, Cinderella!

Instead, Cinderella had to make dresses *for* her stepsisters. "**More *frills!***" they demanded. "**More *flounces!***"

On the day of the ball, the stepsisters gazed at themselves in the mirror.

"Aren't we beautiful?" they said.

That evening, they called for their carriage to take them to the ball.
Ha! Ha! You're not coming!

After they'd gone, Cinderella sat down by the fire and wept. But before long, a fairy appeared, in a shower of sparkles.

"First," said the Fairy Godmother, "I need you to find me a pumpkin."

Cinderella ran to the garden
and picked the BIGGEST,
PLUMPEST pumpkin
she could *find*.

"Now for a little MAGIC!" said the Fairy Godmother.

The Fairy Godmother waved her wand and, in a shower of sparkles, the pumpkin turned into a golden coach.

Six white mice became...

six white horses...

The lizards behind the watering can turned into footmen dressed in green.

Next, was a black rat...

Ping! Ting!

He became a coachman, with long and glossy whiskers.

"And last but not least..."
The Fairy Godmother raised her wand one more time and Cinderella was in the most beautiful ballgown you ever did see.

On her *feet* were a pair of glittering *glass* slippers.

"Now you may go to the ball," said the Fairy Godmother.

"Just remember! Be back by midnight."

"Thank you!" cried Cinderella.
The horses began to prance, the coachman
lifted the reins, and the next moment,
Cinderella was *swept* away to the ball.

When she arrived at the palace,
she walked up the steps
as if in a dream.

"Who is that girl?" everyone said. "She looks so happy. Perhaps she's a princess from a far-off land."

"Will you dance with me?" asked the prince.

Cinderella placed her hand in his, and they glided across the ballroom.

“Oh no!” cried Cinderella’s stepsisters.
“We wanted to dance with the prince!”

Cinderella wished the dance could last *forever*,
but all too soon the clock struck midnight.
She ran *from* the ballroom.

Her dress turned back to rags.
Her carriage was a pumpkin.
Her coachman was a rat.

The prince rushed after her. But all that was left was a glass slipper, glittering on the palace steps.

The prince longed to find the mystery girl who had danced herself into his dreams.

He searched the land, declaring, "I'll marry the girl who *fits* this *shoe!*"

At last, he came to Cinderella's house. The stepsisters **squished** and **squeezed** and **squirmed** and **screamed**...

...but couldn't *fit* their *feet* into the shoe.

"May I try it on?" asked Cinderella.
"NO!" snapped her stepmother. But it was too late.
The shoe was a perfect fit. Cinderella pulled
the other shoe from her pocket...

At once, the room sparkled with stars and Cinderella was dressed in her ballgown once more.

"At last," said the prince. "I've *found* you."

They were married
soon after.

Everyone came to the wedding. Even the **horrid** stepmother and the two **grisly** stepsisters.

As for Cinderella...

did she live *happily* ever after?

YES, she *did!*

The Princess and the Pea

Long ago, and far away,
there lived a prince
who loved adventures.

His name was **Percival.**

He battled fire-breathing dragons...

...scaled mountains and galloped across dusty deserts.

But he always rode home **alone**.

"I want to get married,"
Prince Percival told his parents.
"So I can share my adventures."

"But *for* that," said the
king, "you must *find*
a REAL princess."

"How will I know if a princess IS real?" asked Prince Percival.

"Aha!" replied the king. "You must ask the best inventors in the kingdom, of course."

The *inventors* worked all day and all night, until one cried, "EUREKA! I have *found* a solution!"

She took Prince Percival to the **biggest**, **grandest** room in the palace.

The curtain was pulled back to reveal a

teetering, tottering tower

of mattresses.

"A REAL princess notices everything," said the inventor.

"Even a tiny pea at the bottom of this teetering, tottering pile of mattresses."

After that, the race was on.

Royal messengers set out around the world,

inviting princesses everywhere to take the test.

Princesses came from the icy
wastes of the Arctic...

...from the mountains of Switzerland...

...the deserts of Arabia...

...and *from* India,
journeying under
the burning *sun*.

They came through the *gleaming gates* of the palace in carriage after carriage.

And then the princesses partied the night away, *singing*, dancing and laughing.

One by one,
they took the
REAL
PRINCESS
TEST.

And one
by one,
they
failed.

"What a wonderful night's *sleep!*"
the *princesses* declared.

Not a *single* one of them had noticed
THE PEA.

After the last princess had left, Prince Percival sat at the breakfast table, looking glum.

I don't think I'll ever
find a real princess.

That night, a wild storm shook the palace.
The thunder **crackled** and the lightning ***flashed***.

Rain lashed at the windows. Suddenly, there came a **KNOCK! KNOCK! KNOCK!**

Slowly, the prince opened the door...

There stood a girl, shivering in the cold. "I have nowhere else to go," she said. "Please, may I stay here?"

"Of course," said Prince Percival. "Follow me!"

Our palace is always open to those in need.

They sat by the fire, sharing stories of their adventures.

Finally, Prince Percival's eyes closed... and he fell *fast* asleep.

When he woke, he was alone by the dying embers of the *fire*.

But then... the girl walked in.

"Good morning, sleepy head!" she said.

"Where have you been?" asked the prince.

"After you fell asleep, I looked for a bed – and I found one, as tall as a house!"

"And how did you sleep?" asked Prince Percival.

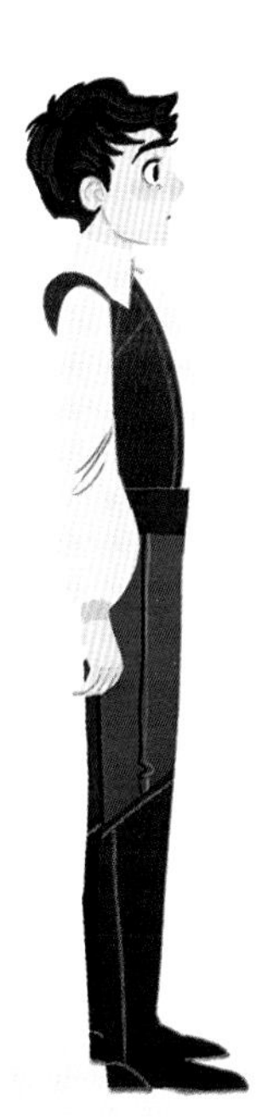

"Well, with all those mattresses, I thought I was going to be so comfortable.

But I didn't get a wink of sleep ALL NIGHT."

"Then you must be a REAL princess!" gasped Prince Percival.

"Because a real princess notices everything," said the prince. And he showed her the pea.

"I've been looking *for* a real princess all this while," said the prince.

The princess laughed.

"And I've been looking for a REAL prince."

"I knew that a real prince would be kind enough to take in a stranger. I've been from palace to palace..."

"You're the only prince who let me in."

They were married that *summer*. It was the beginning of their life *of* adventure together.

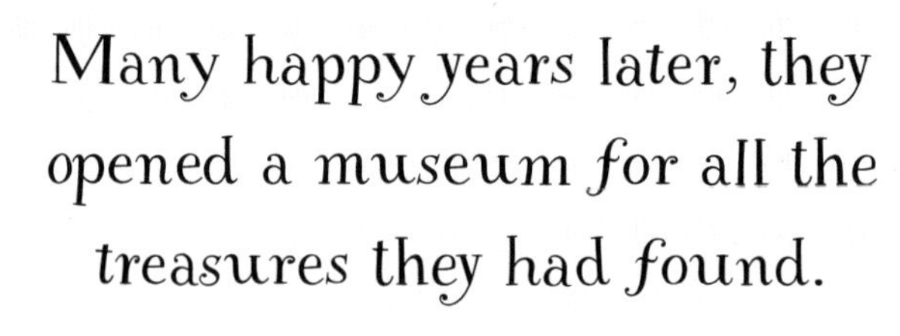

Many happy years later, they opened a museum *for* all the treasures they had *found*.

In pride of place sat the Royal Pea,
on a cushion of royal velvet.

It may still be there today...

With thanks to Rob Lloyd Jones, Anna Milbourne,
Matthew Oldham and Russell Punter

Designed by Laura Nelson Norris
Edited by Lesley Sims

Digital imaging: Mike Olley, Will Dawes,
John Russell and Nick Wakeford

First published in 2018 by Usborne Publishing Ltd., 83-85 Saffron Hill, London EC1N 8RT, England.
www.usborne.com.
UE. First published in America in 2018.